Tolee's Rhyme Time

adapted by Catherine Lukas   based on a screenplay by Bradley Zweig

illustrated by Kellee Riley

Ready-to-Read

SIMON SPOTLIGHT/NICKELODEON
New York   London   Toronto   Sydney

Based on the TV series *Ni Hao, Kai-lan!*™ as seen on Nick Jr.®

SIMON SPOTLIGHT
An imprint of Simon & Schuster Children's Publishing Division
1230 Avenue of the Americas, New York, New York 10020
© 2009 Viacom International Inc. All Rights Reserved. NICKELODEON, *Ni Hao, Kai-lan!*,
and all related titles, logos and characters are trademarks of Viacom International Inc.
All rights reserved, including the right of reproduction in whole or in part in any form.
SIMON SPOTLIGHT, READY-TO-READ, and colophon are registered trademarks of Simon & Schuster, Inc.
For information about special discounts for bulk purchases,
please contact Simon & Schuster Special Sales at 1-866-506-1949 or business@simonandschuster.com.
Manufactured in the United States of America
2 4 6 8 10 9 7 5 3
Library of Congress Cataloging-in-Publication Data
Lukas, Catherine.
Tolee's rhyme time / adapted by Catherine Lukas; illustrated by Kellee Riley. — 1st ed.
p. cm. — (Ready-to-read)
"Based on the TV series Ni Hao, Kai-lan as seen on Nickelodeon"—Copr. p.
ISBN 978-1-4169-9024-6
I. Riley, Kellee, ill. II. Ni Hao Kai-lan (Television program) III. Title.
PZ7.L97822To 2009
[E]—dc22
2009005821

"Ni hao! I am !
KAI-LAN

Watch me toss my
TAMBOURINE

from one  to the other!"
HAND

CRASH!

"I hear music!" says .
KAI-LAN

"  is playing the !
MR. SUN   TRUMPET

The  are playing
LADYBUGS

a ."
PIPA

 **KAI-LAN** has an idea.

"We can have a music show!

Music show, let's go, go, go!"

 asks her friends

KAI-LAN

to play in the show.

 wants to play

RINTOO

the  .

XYLOPHONE

"Roar!" says .
RINTOO

"I love music shows!"

 wants to play

HOHO

his  .

TURNTABLES

They make a

scritch-scratch sound.

TOLEE wants to sing.

"La! La! La!" sings TOLEE.

KAI-LAN wants to try tossing

her TAMBOURINE again.

CLANG!

"Oops!" says KAI-LAN.

"I have to keep trying!"

"What should I sing in our show?" asks .

TOLEE

"How about a song that rhymes?" says .

KAI-LAN

"What is a rhyme?" asks  .

TOLEE

"A rhyme is 2 words

TWO

that sound the same,"

says , "like and ."

KAI-LAN   HOSE   ROSE

tries to rhyme.

TOLEE

" . . . ?"  frowns.

ROCK   CLOUD   TOLEE

"I am no good at rhymes!"

"Keep trying!" says .

KAI-LAN

 tries again.

TOLEE

" . . . ?"

LOG   LEAF

 frowns.
TOLEE

"Rhyming is hard!"  says.
TOLEE

"Do not give up!" says .
KAI-LAN

 thinks hard.
TOLEE

"Hmm.  . . .  ?
FROG TREE

 . . .  ?"
LOG GRASS

 stomps away.
TOLEE

"Rhyming is too hard!
I quit!" TOLEE says.

 hurries over

KAI-LAN

to her friend.

"I know you can do it,

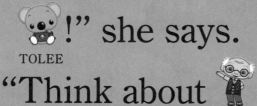!" she says.

TOLEE

"Think about !

YEYE

 YEYE is very good at tai chi.
But to become that good,
he had to practice.
He practiced every day!"

 thinks about .

TOLEE YEYE

 tries again.

TOLEE

"  . . .  .  . . .  !"

LOG FROG BEE TREE

"Great, !" says .

TOLEE KAI-LAN

"And now it is time for the

show!"

The show begins.  tosses the ⊙ .

KAI-LAN

TAMBOURINE

"Hurray! And now 🐨 will

TOLEE

sing a rhyming song!"

"**1, 2, 3.**
ONE TWO THREE

Ni hao! My name is !
TOLEE

I tried and tried to rhyme.

Now I do it all the time!

So don't give up.

 You will see why.

You will get better

if you try, try, try!"

The crowd tosses .

"Good job!" says .

smiles and waves

good-bye.